AMBER THOMA

REALMS OF LORE: FAE

The Fae
Master Uxbridge's Cave
Nocturia Mountains
Nightfell
Borderlands
The Falls
Lunarmist
Ebonmere
Night Court
Cresctaria

Realm
Solarath
Falling Star Coven
r Crystal Coven
lowed Crescent Coven
Daybreak
Day Court
Silver Moon Coven
Mystic Fate Coven
Flarimmar
Coven of Remembrance
Anin's Village
Temple
k Cauldron Coven
Southern Day Court

*To every little girl who was told
to ignore their intuition.*

Dear Reader,

This story might be tiny but it packs a mighty punch and will be triggering to some. Please always consider your own mental health before going into a book. I hope this story can give you some insight and maybe compassion for our Golden/Blood Queen. She experienced things no little girl should and was failed by those meant to protect her. Villains are made, and this is the making of Tatiana's villain era.

Welcome back to the realm,

Amber Thoma

This book contains scenes that may depict, mention, or discuss: abusive relationship, anxiety, assault, blood, bullying, child abuse, emotional abuse, misogyny, pedophilia, physical abuse, poisoning, PTSD, rape, sexual abuse, sexual assault, violence, and other mental health issues. Please read at your own discretion.

SHADOWS
OF
LIGHT
TATIANA

AUTHOR AMBER THOMA

REALMS OF LORE: FAE

READING ORDER:

Prince of Darkness

Heirs of Darkness

Queen of Light

Shadows of Light

Shadows of Light

A Queen of Light Novella

Amber Thoma

"Tatiana!" Glasga yells for me. "Come here, my sweet golden princess." She sweeps me up in her soft furry arms and holds me tight. Glasga has been my nanny since I came into the realm. Not everyone in the palace is nice to her, and I do not understand why. I love her. Sometimes even more than mother, but I would never tell anyone that.

"Your mother has requested your presence in the throne room to sit with her while she holds court." My nose scrunches and I wiggle out of her embrace to make a run for it. She steps in front of me and blocks my escape route.

"I do not want to go! It is always so boring!" She looks at me with her kind eyes and I sigh, knowing I will in fact be sitting in the boring throne room listening to the boring members of this court. "Can I at least bring one of my dolls?" I ask her while giving her a look I have perfected for these exact moments. I make my eyes wide and fill my face with all the hope in the realm.

"I do not see why not. Which one will you pick?" She smiles at me. The sight always makes me feel fuzzy in my chest. The shelves of dolls grew larger every year.

"I wish I had a little sister. We could play with these dolls together. Do you think mother and father would get me a little sister if I am very good?" I think a little sister would be a lot like having another doll, but alive! How wonderful that would be.

Although, every time I ask Glasga about a little sister, her face falls the smallest amount, and she always gives me the same answer.

"I am afraid that is something I do not have the answer to, my darling girl." I knew that was exactly what she was going to say. Sighing, I examine the wall of dolls again and pick the one that has black eyes just like mine. I can pretend that she is my little sister for the day.

Glasga dresses me in one of the gowns my mother prefers I wear when she is holding court. I hate them. They are so… big. I cannot even climb a tree in them. Trust me, I tried. Mother was not very happy with me that day.

I had enough of sitting there pretending to have even the slightest idea of what was being discussed. I had already grown bored with trying to come up with silly stories for all the fae in the room based solely on what they were wearing. I had gotten up and ran for the door hidden behind the throne and made a break for the trees where I knew my friends would be.

I ripped so many layers off of that dress—not unlike the one Glasga laces me into now—before I could shimmy my way up the trunk of the tree. No one came to fetch me back, so I stayed out all day with my friends. When I grew tired and hungry, I returned to my quarters to find the door cracked open and my father yelling at Glasga just before he struck her across the face.

I had been so shocked, why would anyone dream of hurting my dear sweet nanny? But then I heard him say, "If you cannot keep track of my daughter, then you are of no use to anyone and I will sell your deal to another." She kept her head down and said nothing until my father stormed out of the room to find me standing there wide eyed.

He smiled at me as if he had not just hurt the being I cherished most in the realm and said, "Ah, there you are, my little golden ray. We have been looking for you." He stopped and took in the state of my dress and chuckled. "Do not let your mother see the way you redesigned your gown." He winked at me before he strolled down the hall, whistling no less.

I ran into the room and wrapped my arms as far around my nanny as I could and cried, telling her how sorry I was. I promised her I would never sneak away from her again. A fae's promise is not something to be taken lightly and I remember the way she sucked in a shocked gasp.

"Oh, my sweet girl. I release you of your promise. You did nothing but behave exactly the way any youngling should." It did not matter that she did not take the promise, I have still held true to it. The memory compels me to spin and wrap my tiny arms around her ample waist and squeeze as tight as I can.

"Now, what's all this?" Glasga asks while laughing and leaning forward to kiss the top of my head.

"Can I not hug my favorite nanny?" I ask with a fake pout that only makes her laugh harder. The sound bubbles out from her gut and causes her whole body to shake with each laugh.

I must always enter the throne room through the side entrance so that I can be seen, yet not be disruptive. At least that is the reason my mother gave me when I asked why I had to come through that exact door. Just as Glasga's hand fell to the knob, Reminold appears. He is my mother's advisor and friend of my parents. I do not know why, but something about him makes me feel like I have creepy crawlies under my skin.

"Tatiana, my favorite little heart breaker. You are a vision of a female today. I will have to fight off all the males as I escort you to your mother," he says, taking my small hand in his big one. I do not like it when he touches me. I give Glasga a pleading look.

When she tries to interject, Reminold's too bright smile falls. "Begone lesser before you do something you will live to regret." Her gaze drops to mine and tears fill her eyes. I give her a smile, trying to tell her I can handle it on my own. That is until he rips the doll out of my hand and tosses it to her.

I cry out, and he squeezes my hand too tight and tells me I am much too old to be acting like a youngling. I give Glasga a confused look. I am only twelve years old and very much a youngling.

When my lower lip trembles, he glares at me and squeezes my hand just a little bit harder, a threat even my young mind can understand.

Behave or else.

I do not think I will ever forget the look my nanny wears as she stares at where my hand disappears into his. It reflects the way I feel inside.

When the door opens, he drops my hand and places his arm across my shoulders before draping his large, white, downy wings around us, forcing me to walk even closer to him. He has a strange smell about him, slightly sour, that always makes my nose crinkle. I do not know how anyone can stand to be near him.

I look straight ahead at my mother and count down the steps until I am sitting next to her and free of him. However, when we reach the dais, he climbs the stairs with me and my mother shifts her gaze toward us, giving him a warm smile before inspecting me for any flaws.

"Do you require my assistance further, my queen?" he asks her in a voice that drips down my spine.

"Oh Reminold, please do stay. Your insight is always appreciated," she says, but then lowers her voice so only we can hear. "I have one of those headaches again." He nods and pulls out a small bottle. He blocks her chalice before pouring a small amount of the contents into her drink. The concoction reminds me of the sour smell that seems to coat him.

He takes a seat in the chair I usually occupy while I stand there, uncertain as to where I am supposed to sit. I really do not want to stand the entire time.

"Come, Tatiana," he says, patting his lap before pulling me on to it and resting his hands on my knees.

On second thought, standing would not have been so bad.

"Tatiana?"

"What? Can you repeat the question?" I asked my tutor. He's a high fae with a funny shaped nose. I stopped learning their names after the first few days. Since every day there is a new tutor. When I asked mother why, she said it was advised to make sure that no inappropriate attachments were formed.

I assumed she meant like I had with Glasga. It was not long after she attempted to come between me and Raindal that she simply disappeared. There was no goodbye, no visits. She left me. The one being I felt I could be myself around and say anything to, left me. She had made me feel safe, and she was the only being who noticed if I was sad or uncomfortable and tried to do something about it.

And she just left me.

I forced myself to stop thinking of her a couple of

years ago. Everyone told me lesser fae were not trust-worthy and were lesser for a reason. I had never believed it. I was Glasga's number one concern. Not the court, the realm, or appearances—me. Until I was not, and she walked away from me without the slightest regard for my feelings. I will never make the same mistake of thinking higher of a lesser fae.

My general studies ended a few weeks ago, and I started the required studies for a queen. It's interesting enough, and I am told I am quite good at them. However, I am not sure what they have to go off of since the tutor changes daily. How do they know if I am improving? What scale do they have to measure my success?

"I did not ask you a question. I told you a few times class was over," funny nose says. I find myself staring out the windows of the study more often than I look at the stacks of books and scrolls in front of me. I am always searching for the sight of one of my friends running by.

I see them out there from time to time. None of them seem to miss me, yet that did not prevent me from missing them. Twenty years old is still far too young to be expected to sit still all day. I need to run, jump, and climb trees. I miss the way the sun felt on my skin. By the time my daily studies come to an end, eclipse day is coming, and the sun does not feel half as warm.

"I would say I would see you tomorrow, but I won't. Good day." The fae male did not seem to know what to say, and his nose did a silly little dance on his face as his features pulled together in discomfort.

He's lucky, though. In the beginning I asked the first several fae tasked with teaching me how to rule this court why they would never return. It was a question that seemed to make them entirely too uncomfortable for such a simple one, and not a single one of them ever gave me an answer. Instead, they only suggested I speak with the queen, my mother, about that.

I know Reminold has something to do with it. I have no idea why he enjoys tormenting me the way he does. I wonder if it's because I will someday be his queen and he will have to listen to what I say. If that's the case, he is rather unintelligent because, as of now, I want nothing more than to make his life miserable when I take the throne.

Each time I try to speak to my mother about his behavior, but it never goes well. This last time was possibly the most absurd yet.

"Mother, this is getting ridiculous, do you not think? Does *he* have something to do with my never ending line of daily tutors?" I asked, seething.

"And who would this mysterious 'he' be, my sweet?" she asked. Her tone was confusingly conspiratorial.

"Reminold," I spat, and she laughed at me. Laughed!

"Oh, my sweet ray of sunshine, there is no reason to feel embarrassed," she said, patting my hand.

"What do you mean? Why would I be embarrassed?"

"Your fascination with Reminold is well known amongst all the high fae. It is perfectly normal for a youngling of your age to fancy an older male." She smiled as if we were sharing a joke that only the two of us would understand. Although she seemed to be the only one in on it.

"Mother, I do not have a *fascination* with Reminold. If anything, I despise him." I could only stare with openmouthed disbelief at her next words.

"Tatiana, you do not need to lie to me. He is quite handsome and every young girl needs a male to set their sights on. Is there nothing more enjoyable than the thrill of being smitten?"

There was no use telling her I had no idea and that it seemed like she was the one with the infatuation. Has she forgotten that I am only twenty years old? I find dolls more entertaining than males. Particularly old males that are friends with my parents.

I know I am alone in this strange war he has manufactured between us. No one, besides Glasga, has ever noticed the way he pinches me or squeezes my hand too tight. She had been the only one to hear the thinly veiled threats he made against me. But she left me, and now I am alone.

My friends have been my only safe space after Glasga. They are the only beings I feel like I can still be myself with. With them, nothing else matters besides who can win the next race or who can steal a sun cake from the palace baker without being caught. It's easy to forget, for the few hours I spent with them, how the rest of my life seems to happen to me. Without even being an active participant. I always feel like I am a step behind.

I may be twenty, but I swear this game he forced upon me makes me feel closer to a century and I am already tired. I look out the window again as the tutor and his funny nose look anywhere but at me. I am sure he has no idea what to do if I do not immediately leave after class.

I just want to catch a glimpse of my friends. I wonder what they are doing right at this very moment. Are they climbing trees in our favorite grove? Perhaps they are at one of the lakes we—well, they—frequent. I can not remember the last time I felt the sun bake my skin as we lay on the shore, letting the heat dry our clothes. Wherever they are, I hope they are having far more fun than I am, maybe even having enough for me.

The tutor I will never see again clears his throat, and I glance back at him, sighing. I do not bother collecting any of the items on the table. They will all be there tomorrow. The only thing that will change is the being that teaches me.

I wonder what would happen if I simply did not show up. Perhaps I will find out tomorrow.

Of Despair & Bondings

It happened. I am now bonded to the prince of the Night Court and I could not be more miserable for it.

I assumed I would have no say in the ceremony itself, considering I had no say in participating in it. What I had not been expecting was to do it completely alone. Not a single member of my family had been permitted to attend. Not even my mother to sit with me while I waited for my impending doom in the Queen's Suite.

I could tell the rooms had not been used for several years. There was no collection of dust or any other indication of neglect. The place was spotless. However, rooms that sit empty for too long lose the echoes of the beings that used to frequent them. You might not see them, but you can feel the memory life leaves behind.

I should not be surprised. This palace does not inspire life. If anything, it sucks it away. I fear for the life I will have locked behind these walls. I just hope I can see my family soon because it has only been three nights and I already miss them all terribly.

Even the Chronicler, a tree like being impartial to all events and only there to record the history of the realms, understood I was being forced into this union. When they spoke directly into my mind and told me they had documented the truth of the event and not just what the king and prince wanted history to reflect. I was grateful. In that brief moment, I did not feel so alone. How funny that I felt the most compassion and warmth from a being such as that. I can not say the same for any others in attendance.

It angers me that I still have tears to shed over my new life. I do not want to give him the satisfaction of knowing he has caused me pain. I know he would enjoy it far too much. I suppose I should feel lucky that he has not once come to my room or sought me out to demand his rights as my bonded. I dread the night that comes.

With despair,
Dealla, Princess of the Night Court

I *hate* dealing with the gods. They love nothing more than to make the rest of us feel inferior. I have been waiting at the meeting place he chose in the Human Realm for hours now. There is not much time left before the veil closes and I am stuck here till the next one opens.

If I did not need what he can give me so badly, then I would have already left. This is the only way I can get what I want. It's more than a want, it's what I am *owed*. I have served the crown for long enough. It's *my* turn to be served.

The place he chose is the ruins of a long forgotten circle of stones the idiotic humans used to worship the gods at. I would like nothing more than to mock them for practically begging for favor from whatever gods they prayed to. Yet here I am, about to do the exact same thing.

If he even shows.

He better show. The timing has to be just right, and I have been meticulously planning this moment for decades—*centuries*, even. I made myself important to the queen when she was the queen in waiting. I will be honest, at the time I had been attempting to tie myself to her. It was shortsighted and impractical to expect such an outcome. Her parents chose that imbecile that sits on the throne next to her.

She would have chosen me. I have no doubts. I have warmed her bed on many occasions. Not that it is anything to brag about.

There are not many males in the entire realm who have not known the touch of the Day Queen. She is even fond of taking the Night King to her bed. He apparently has a specific need that she is all too happy to fulfill. He's careful to never say anything negative about her, likely out of fear she will share his dirty little secrets.

I tried to get her to tell me. Knowledge is power, after all. She giggled and told me a queen never kisses and tells. None of the information and leverage she has gleaned between the sheets is something she will ever give up to anyone. I even tried to fuck it out of her, not that it was a hardship.

There is not a single place I have not explored on the queen, nor is there a hole I have not claimed. While I am one of many for her, if my plans all come together, I will own every inch of her daughter and will be the first and last one to claim her body.

Her youth excites me. While her body is not as desirable as her mother's yet, the control I am able to exact on her is addictive. The way she fights me only makes me desire her little body even more. She will be mine and I will control her and therefore I will control the court.

With the queen's illness beginning to weaken her, it won't be long until she is removed from the picture. It makes me want to laugh every time she asks for help with her headaches. Each time I pour her tincture into her cup is one day closer to her death. I cannot believe she has not thought her decline and the fix I alone have for her headache are related.

The king, on the other hand, was not as easy to figure out, which is shocking considering what an *idiot* he is. I finally found his downfall. The king enjoys the fae wine a little too much and, with a little encouragement and regularity, it is not often you see him without a glass of wine in one hand. Recently, I have encouraged him to go and explore the court. He should not be shackled to the palace simply because he is bonded to the queen.

"You are looking mighty smug for a fae," says a lilting voice from a shadow cast by a tall stone. The god steps out, clearly pleased to find me still waiting for him. "Well, what is it? Do not keep me waiting on you."

It takes everything within me to swallow down the retort I desperately want to spew at him. Who, exactly, had been keeping who waiting? I clench my jaw together till it aches and the god's grin only grows larger.

"I wish to make a deal."

"Obviously," he says, his grin dropping slightly. I can not let him get bored or there is no chance he is going to stay long enough to even hear me out.

"I wish to trick fate." The god's eyes grow wide and his grin returns.

"You wish for the sun and the moon of all the realms. I can appreciate your ambition. Say I desired to have a little fun with fate. What do I get in return?"

This is where it gets dangerous for me. Offer too much and all of this hard work will be for nothing, offer too little and the god will disappear without a word. The last thing I want is to offend a god.

"A favor."

"A favor to be called upon at any time," he counters.

"A favor to be called upon at any time after one thousand years." It's a bold bet to make, but what is a thousand years to a god?

"I do enjoy being owed favors. Do you know what I enjoy more?" he asks.

"I would imagine many things, but what do you, in this moment, enjoy more?" The god lets out a shrill laugh, and I have to fight the muscles in my own face to keep from revealing just how horrible of a sound it is.

"You are quite right. There are many things I do enjoy more. However, when it comes to being owed a favor, I enjoy showing up at the least convenient times and reminding you that you are indebted to a god and what the possible favors are that I could call in. It is great fun watching the color drain from beings' faces as they contemplate whether the deal was worth it."

"It is worth it."

"I imagine so if you wish to trick fate. Sounds fun, I agree."

"Do you not want to know what it is that I desire?"

"I have no doubts you will tell me. Whatever it is, consider it done." I no longer try to control my expression and allow a smile to stretch my face, knowing this is the moment that I won.

"I want to be the fated mate of the Day Queen's daughter, Tatiana." The god releases another one of his horrific laughs that echo out into the night. The sound grates across my mind and nerves. The longer it goes on, the harder it becomes to keep the victorious smile adorning my face.

"Oh, that is truly *disgusting*. Is she not still a youngling?" I glare at the god, which only makes him laugh again. "You should see your face right now. Do not worry, you sick bastard. I love the chaos this will cause."

The god is upon me faster than should be possible. He is nothing but a blur as he comes to stand before me and reaches into my chest. The sight of his hand disappearing inside my ribcage nearly makes me vomit. The next second, the god flickers out of sight, only to reappear a moment later.

"I will be watching all of this unfold. I imagine she will be beyond confused if I interpreted her feelings about you correctly. She detests you. Do you know that?" I stare at the god for one... two... three heartbeats as I let what he said sink into the marrow of my bones. I could not care less if she hates me as long as I become the king and have absolute control over the queen.

"It's done?"

"It's done." I want nothing more than to scream and shout in celebration, but I only allow myself to nod and return to the soon-to-be closing veil. As soon as I am back in my own realm, I lift my face to the eclipsed sun and feel the weight of so many moving pieces dissipate as they all fall into place.

Tomorrow Tatiana is *mine*.

Chapter 4
Tatiana

A Horrifying Bond

When I woke up today, I thought it was going to be much the same as every other day in my mundane life. I would have lessons with a new stranger while gazing out the window, searching for sightings of my friends.

Recently I have begun to wonder—-well, more like obsess over—-if they miss me as much, or even a fraction as much, as I miss them. Not a single one of them has come to visit me since our studies went in different directions several years ago. It makes me question if any of them have ever truly been my friend from the start.

Not that it matters; everyone I seem to care about abandons me at some point, while the beings I wish would leave seem to only come around more often. Namely Reminold, who is always quick to point out that no one truly cares for me. He has been the one to point out that my friends likely only befriended me because I will be queen one day. Perhaps he is right.

Imagine my horror when he enters the throne room while I sit next to my mother listening to the Day fae drone on about one thing or another and feel something snap into place within my chest at the first sight of him. My mother has rarely mentioned what a mate bond is. If it had not been for Glasga telling me fanciful stories about true love when I was barely knee high, I might have thought nothing of it. As it is, dread pools heavily in my gut for what feels like exactly what my traitorous nanny had described. If only I had ported away, or never came when my mother called for me, I could live several more hours in peace.

"Princess, it seems today calls for a celebration." I find it odd that is the first thing he says to me. There is no surprise or wonder on his face. He did not react at all. Meanwhile, I wish for nothing more than to shrivel up and return to the realm. Surely, a second chance at life would be preferable to being mated to *him* of all beings.

The shock of not only being mated but also whom I am mated to becomes too much. I am certain you are supposed to feel elated and in awe of your mate when the bond first takes root. The only thing I feel is revulsion.

I am far too young to be mated. I have to be. I am still decades away from no longer being considered a youngling.

I do not know how long I sit there, staring at him in horror while he smiles at me with smug satisfaction. I knew fate could be cruel, but I had no idea she could be this sadistic.

My fated mate is my tormentor.

I can no longer pull air into my lungs, and my body feels both hot and cold as he approaches me. My head begins to buzz from the lack of air, and I feel myself sway before everything turns black. A plea to the gods, my last thought.

"Gods, please no."

———

"...Underful news! Oh look, she's coming back around." I can smell the familiar scent of daisies warmed by the sun all around me before I feel my mother's hand stroking my hair. "You must have been so overcome with joy, my beautiful ray of sunshine," she says to me.

My heart immediately begins to race, the sound drowning out any other words that might be spoken. For one brief moment, I forgot the burden fate has bestowed upon me.

"Mother..." the word comes out in a shaking breath. "I am too young, right? There must be some kind of mistake." I look at her with so much hope, my eyes pleading with her to save me just this once.

"Fate does not make mistakes, my little one. This is a joyous occasion and calls for a celebration! I cannot recall the last time there was a fated pair on the throne of the Day Court." I do not know why I expect anything else from her. She has never seen him the way I do. Only Glasga had.

My eyes clash with my apparent mate and I cannot help the tear that escapes down my cheek. "But mother, he is so very old." She just laughs along with everyone else in the room. I only just remembered we are in the throne room and I am laid across my mother's lap like I used to do when I needed comforting. While I have grown quite a bit since then, I am still small enough, at least for now. Although nothing can comfort the turmoil inside me.

I know there are several sets of eyes in the room staring at me, and yet I can only feel one pair. I refuse to meet them again. Perhaps I can elude him for an eternity.

"We should begin planning the bonding ceremony," Reminold says. A chill steals down my spine as the word "no" plays on a constant loop inside my mind. There is obviously no point in voicing my rejection of the bond. If my own mother will not hear it, I know there is no way Reminold will.

"Nonsense. There is no rush, and she is still far from reaching maturity," my mother says, waving her hand dismissively and my lungs—while slow—fill fully for the first time since the dreadful bond made its presence known. I allow myself to glance at him once more and I immediately wish I had not. His eyes hold a dangerous determination, and I know he has a way of easily swaying my mother's fickle mind.

———

Weeks later, I once again sit in front of a stranger who attempts to teach me a long dead language that I wonder if I will ever need. It does not matter, however, I will learn everything I can no matter the subject. *He* never bothers me during my studies.

I glance out the large windows and nearly gasp when I see a group of my friends running toward the palace gardens with the best trees to climb. The fae tutor follows my gaze and lets out a sigh. I look at her, expecting annoyance, only to be surprised at the soft smile she gives me.

"You have the rest of your life to learn how to be a queen, but you only have so many decades left of being a youngling. Go find your friends," she says and her words make tears well in my eyes. It has been so long since someone recognized my youth. "Please, do me the favor of asking your parents first. I would hate to find myself on the receiving end of their ire."

I assure her I will as I flee the room and begin porting to all the locations in the palace that I can be sure to find one of my parents. I finally find them in my mother's lounge and stop short when I find them with Reminold.

"My little sun ray, what are you doing here? Are you not meant to be in your studies?" my mother asks.

"She said as long as you allowed it I could go and play with my friends since I only have a few more decades of being a youngling," I responded, excitement dripping from every word. I am finally going to get to see my friends again.

My mother smiles and begins to nod, but before a word can pass her lips, *he* interjects.

"That is not a good idea, my little mate," he says, as if I am his possession. I have no doubt that is exactly how he sees me. "What if you were to get injured?"

I roll my eyes and am about to remind him of how I heal quite quickly. Beyond that, my elemental magic is a golden healing light. I am often the one healing my friends. There have been a few wounds that would have taken months to regrow all the way, yet I was able to make it so they could go home without their parents ever knowing how careless their youngling could be. It might not be as flashy as normal elemental powers, but it is something no one else has.

"And you need to be smarter than any other queen to make up for your lack of a powerful element." I blink a few times, making sure I heard him correctly.

Did he just say my magic was not powerful?

Before I can respond to his ridiculous notion, my mother and father are nodding in agreement. Do they think my magic is weak as well?

"I am sorry, little ray, he is your mate, and he makes a good point. Run along back to your studies," my mother says, dismissing me.

She and my father turn back to whatever document they were examining, but Reminold waits for me to meet his gaze. He wants me to see the wicked smile he wears. I know he enjoys hurting me and I cannot understand why. He is the mate fate chose for me and he is supposed to love me more than anyone else. If that were true, then why does he seem to gain so much pleasure from my misery?

I port back to the study where my tutor still sat waiting to hear the verdict. She already cleaned the space and put all the books away. Her smile falls when she sees my face. I shake my head and take my seat.

"That is a shame; I am sorry, princess." The words are said with such kindness that it is a struggle to keep the tears threatening to fall locked up tight.

I let myself glance out the window one last time for the day. A mistake. Watching my friends climbing trees, certain I am never going to be that free ever again, makes me lose the battle with my tears.

Dealla

Of Loneliness & Misery

There are no words to express how much I hate it here. No one speaks to me, no one even allows me to approach them. I am certain it is by design. What I am not certain of is why. What purpose does it serve?

I have not been able to communicate with my family in decades. Spelled scrolls do not come in or out of the palace, at least not for me. My tears ran dry not long after becoming a princess, and I despise the bitter female I am becoming. I can feel the essence of who I used to be slipping away every night. The memory of what joy felt like is comparable to the tune of a song you can no longer recall, but the echo it leaves lingers just out of reach. Perhaps it is for the best. I cannot miss what I do not remember.

The funny thing is, I am far stronger than the prince and yet he still, somehow, leashed me. Even with this deep well of power, I am powerless. I cannot even get my shadows to move beyond the walls of the palace. While there is no way of knowing how he does it, it's obvious powerful magic is at play.

The king is unwell. He is a cruel male who managed to raise an even crueler son. They are both afflicted with some disease of the mind and I think it has finally taken its toll on the king. He has suddenly started aging at an accelerated rate and, if he continues, I strongly doubt he has more than a handful of decades left to live. Relatively speaking, he is young for a king. I can only hope his son's lifespan follows the same trend.

That is my only hope for freedom. Spite alone fuels the desire to outlive him. On the rare occasion we have any interaction, I make sure to tell him he will not control me forever. He can do nothing once he returns to the realm, if the realm even takes his rotten being back.

I know he would love nothing more than to punish me for the way I speak to him, but this is the one thing he cannot control. I am more powerful than him and endeavor to make him regret choosing me as his bonded mate.

I still do not understand why he chose me. He has never touched me, thank the gods. If the bonding ceremony was meant to allow us to share our wells of power, I have closed myself off to him so securely he cannot touch a drop. I honestly do not even know if that is how it is supposed to work, but I am not taking any chances.

It is a miserable existence, having only your rage to keep you company. I do not wish it on anyone. Well, that simply is not true. I wish the worst of everything for the prince and king. They are everything I have ever wanted to change about the Night fae.

I do not know who suggested all Night fae are evil. What an absurd notion. I am willing to bet it was someone as awful as the prince who was looking to normalize their insanity. Of course there are Night fae who embrace this perceived existence, but I grew up surrounded by kindness.

When I first arrived at the palace, I thought the occupants would be similar to those in the city. I had been so incredibly wrong. The high fae of the court are treacherous while the mixed fae of the city are easy to get along with. Of course, there have been many wicked pranks that perhaps went too far, but the purpose was always a laugh and not misery.

I grow tired of writing the same things about this place. Yet, there is nothing else for me to write about. I am bored, but mostly I am so painfully alone.

Miserably,
Dealla, the ignored princess of the Night Court

Chapter 5
Tatiana
A Time to Grow Up

He is *everywhere*. I cannot even enjoy a simple meal with my parents without his company souring it. Although, these days, any time spent with my parents is not exactly pleasant. While theirs has never been a love match, they have always fostered a strong friendship. They have been kind and supportive of each other. Even if neither of them ever really saw me, I was happy that they were happy.

No one is happy anymore.

Well, no one but Reminold.

My mother's headaches are getting worse and it makes her mood unpredictable. Her patience is short and her words are sharp most of the time. Reminold's elixirs do not seem to help as much as they once had. The strangest part is that her power does not seem to heal whatever is causing the piercing pain behind her tight eyes. Not even my own magic can touch it.

While rare for fae to fall ill, it does happen, usually with deadly results.

I worry for my mother.

It does not help that Reminold and my father tend to stay up far too late drinking fae wine. My father becomes loud and clumsy the more he consumes. His behavior, combined with my mother's illness, has led to them fighting often and bickering constantly. They tried, at first, to keep their animosity from showing in front of me, but they long stopped caring.

Every day, I fear, will be the one where my parents finally relent to *his* constant attempts to persuade them to move forward with the bonding ceremony. I beg the gods daily to take back this wretched mate bond. He is horrible and I do not understand why fate has decided to curse me.

The last time I attempted to see my friends; I had been sitting in the study in front of yet another stranger, paying little attention to what they were saying once I glimpsed my friends streaking across the garden just outside the window. I was not making the mistake of asking this time. I said nothing to the tutor and ported to where I had last seen them running. There are only so many places they could have been going, so I checked the trees first, but there was no sign of them. When I arrived at the lake, *he* was there. My friends were redressing and whatever he said to them had them glaring at me. It was as if they blamed me for ruining their fun.

"Why did you send my friends away?" I

demanded, angry that he had once again prevented me from seeing them.

"They are nothing but a distraction from your studies, and you do not need to be influenced by such imbeciles." His words had stunned me. I had never once questioned their intelligence and was offended on their behalf.

"Those are my friends you speak of!" I screeched at him.

"They are not your friends."

"They have always been my friends!" I stomped my small foot and glared at him. He sighed as if I were nothing but a nuisance.

"Come, little cherub, let's go home." I hate when he calls me that. I hate *him*.

"I am going nowhere with you," I seethed. He moved so quickly and snatched my wrist in his firm grip. The sudden movement startled me. His grip tightened and then he jerked me toward him so hard, a pained cry squeaked out.

"It is time for you to grow up and stop acting like a youngling," he said, glaring down at me.

"But I am a youngling," I stated. How was I supposed to be something I was not?

"No, you are a soon-to-be queen and you are *MY* mate. Now, start making good choices." He pulled me into his face, and I truly feared him for the first time. "Or I will have no choice but to make them for you. Do you understand…. Mate?"

My lower lip had quivered as his grip tightened

further. "Yes," I whispered so softly only fae ears could have heard me.

It is a strange feeling. I hate him; I know I do, and yet it is like false feelings of love are being forced upon me. It is confusing and I know he can feel my emotions through the bond.

He seems to always show up when I am particularly excited. Without fail, it is when I am playing a game or acting out a story I created in my mind with my dolls. Once, I was rather excited over a new outfit that contained my first pair of trousers.

I was imagining how much easier movement would be and how I bet I could finally beat Thatcher in a race up a tree. We are the two fastest climbers out of all our friends, but I have always held a suspicion that it is the layers of fabric tangling between my legs and branches that give him the advantage.

I was sliding the trousers up my legs, clad in nothing but the sheer undergarments that barely hid my developing body when he ported directly into my bedroom, giving me no time to cover myself. I stood there frozen as his eyes raked over every inch of me. An unknown feeling slammed into me from him down the bond that made my skin feel as though it were burning up while my stomach revolted, threatening to release its contents. The combination of sensations coating me with an imaginary layer of filth.

He gave me a smile that seemed to hold a promise that I could not comprehend as he casually strode toward me. Fear prevented me from moving a single muscle even the barest of inches. "What is this, Tatiana?" he asked, gesturing to the trousers I still held halfway up my legs. "A queen does not wear trousers. Take them off." It was a demand, not a request. His voice, low and demanding, made me feel like prey and threatened violence if I did not follow his instructions.

Tears dripped from my chin, landing on the bare skin above my undergarments, reminding me just how vulnerable I was. Without a word, I quickly shed the trousers I would never get to wear and grabbed the dress I had discarded when I attempted to try them on. I held the dress to my chest as if it were a shield that could protect me from his roaming eyes.

He closed the distance and stared down at me, making me feel even more powerless. He wiped my tears away before letting his hands rest on my bare shoulders. "Do not ever let me catch you wearing anything that is not befitting a queen. Do you understand, Tatiana?" I dropped my eyes to the small strip of floor between us and nodded.

"Good girl," he said. His fingers felt like spiders as they crawled down my arms, and then he was gone. I sucked in air before choking on my sobs.

I do not even understand why I was so upset. He is my mate, there is nothing wrong with him seeing me dressing.

Right?

Chapter 6
Tatiana

A Whispered Greeting

I have just turned fifty-two. A fact, it seems, I constantly have to remind everyone. Something I find absurd since with one glance at me it's clear I have not finished growing. My limbs are gangly and I have a habit of tripping over my own feet. My features look too large for my face, making me look even younger than I am. So how is that everyone else around me seems to forget?

The mating ceremony has become a regular topic of conversation, much to my horror. I spend all of my free time in the library and archives looking for any way to break a fated mate bond. So far, all I have found are tragic tales of one mate dying and the other following shortly behind. That crossed killing him off my list. Mostly I have found tales of true love so beautiful they bring me to tears.

There is something *wrong* with my mate bond. I know it. Everything I have read says that a mate bond does not appear until the second century of life. I am just over half the age of the supposed minimum.

They all mention the sharing of each other's wells. However, I cannot feel his at all, yet I feel mine draining faster daily. I know he is stealing my power, but I do not know how to stop it.

"We can show you."

I look up and search the cavernous space of the archives, looking for the owner of the voice. It sounded like several voices at once. However, sound has been known to echo oddly down here.

No one is there. I look between a few rows of shelves, but I seem to be alone.

"Hello?" No one answers me and I shake my head, trying to clear it. Obviously, I only heard what I wished someone would say to me. Clearly, I need to take a break.

Just as I start to close up all the books and return them to their designated places, I feel someone arrive behind me. I do not need to look to know who it is. Everything I have read has told me the icy dread I feel every time *he* is near is not a normal response to one's mate.

"What are you spending all of your time looking for down here, Tatiana?" he asks as he reaches over my shoulder to pick up the first book of the stack sitting on the table in front of me. "Fated Mates: A History. Hmmm." He flips the book open to the first marker I have left in it and reads.

"You would not be trying to do something bad

now, would you, *mate*?" I hate myself for the way my body shakes with fear. I am going to be a queen, and I cannot even face him with a straight spine. Who am I kidding? I cannot even meet his eyes. Over the past couple of years, I have learned it's better to stay silent than to respond at all.

His hand grips the back of my neck and all I can do is try to get more than gasps of breath into my lungs. There is no time. He slams my face onto the table, causing an explosion of pain. I cry out, even though I try my best not to make a sound.

I feel his body lean over mine until his mouth is next to my ear, his hot damp breath on my cheek. "You will never be rid of me, my little golden mate. I will be the king and you will be a weak queen." He holds me there a little longer, making my weakness even more apparent. The pressure on the back of my neck disappears and I am once again alone in the archives.

I fall to the floor, sobbing and clutching my damaged cheek. My magic is already healing the wound. He controls everything I do, everywhere I go, and everyone I see. He has separated me from everyone. Even my parents speak to me through him.

I am so very lonely.

"We can show you how to gain more power than you could ever dream of having. No one could ever touch you again if you did not desire it."

There go my deepest desires speaking to me again. If I ever wondered how lonely I would need to be until I created an imaginary being to converse with, I now knew the answer. What I would not give to keep Reminold from ever laying a hand on me again. Sighing, I pick myself up off the floor and return the books and scrolls to where I found them.

Keeping everything around me orderly gives me a sense of control that I do not have over any other aspect of my life. The palace has lesser fae to keep it, since they could be controlled. Brownies might be preferred for the tidiest outcome, but good luck trying to control them. A few times I have had to rearrange my wall of dolls when they were not put back in the correct spot. I rarely touch them anymore. Every time I do, *he* shows up and tells me to stop acting like a youngling. I think I keep them as a small rebellion at this point.

With all texts back in their places, I leave the archives, doubtful I will find myself back here again. Not now that he is catching on to my search for a way to free myself of him. I thought a fated mate was supposed to enhance your life, not burden it.

"All you need to do is listen to us and we can show you how to take everything you ever wanted. Do you not want to take your life back?" I wish these whispers in my mind were real. There is nothing I desire more than to control my own future.

———

I port to the dining room and take my usual seat. I thought I would be early for dinner, but it looks like my parents and Reminold have already been here for a while. My father's face is ruddy with drink and my mother has that faraway look she gets after consuming the tincture for her headaches. Reminold's eyes are the only ones clear, and the smug satisfaction he wears so easily worries me. Perhaps he is only thinking about our interaction hours ago and I touch my cheek without thought. Still, my stomach flips several times and my palms become so slick my glass cup nearly slides out of my shaking hands.

"There she is, my darling little ray of sunshine," my mother says, eyes still cloudy with pain and whatever is dulling her senses. "We were just discussing you." My heart thunders in my chest to a beat I can only describe as alarm. I do not know what it is about this particular moment, we have had several just like it, but this one makes my head feel uncannily airy.

"You were discussing me without my being present?" I ask, doing my best to hide the fear attempting to strangle my throat closed.

"I suppose we should have called you to be present for the discussion, but it is not something a youngling should concern themselves with." Reminold's smile makes the food in front of me no longer appetizing.

"Which is it? Am I a youngling or not? You all seem to choose which, based upon what suits your needs best," I snap, glaring at Reminold. I know I will live to regret the words, yet at this moment I cannot be bothered to care. Tears of frustration prick my eyes. I am neither a youngling nor a mature fae. I do not know what that makes me.

"Tatiana!" My mother's voice is shocked. "That is no way to talk to the three beings that love you most in the entire realm." If they are the ones that love me most, then why do they cause me the most pain? "For gods' sake, these younglings are so dramatic these days."

They all laugh as if I am not sitting at the same table as them. None of them see me. They never really have. They might see the physical form of me, but they never truly *see* me.

"Tatiana, your mother and I have been speaking with your mate about your upcoming mating ceremony," my father slurs, turning his sloppy smile on me. It takes me two heartbeats to hear what he said.

"My what?" I ask, the question coming out in a whisper, as if my own voice refuses to accept what he said.

"Yes, little cherub, your parents and I just finalized the details for our mating ceremony. You must be so pleased. I know how hard it has been for you to wait these past few years."

What?

"No." This time my voice does not betray me.

"What was that, dear?" my mother asks. I refuse to look at Reminold, and I can feel the promise of violence coming my way through the bond. I do not need to see it reflected in his eyes as well.

I cannot lose my nerve.

This is my last chance.

I can feel it.

"I do not want to have my mating ceremony. It has not been difficult for me to wait. If anything, it has been difficult for me to believe this is a true mate bond. I despise him," I seethe. I put every ounce of hatred I feel towards him into each of my words. If my parents do not hear me now, they never will.

My mother's brow scrunches, and confusion that has nothing to do with her headaches fills her eyes. My father's glass pauses midway to his mouth, and they both look at me. They *heard* me. For once. Hope blooms in my heart while it simultaneously pounds in my chest.

Finally, I am safe.

Reminold throws his head back before a laugh booms out of him. "Oh, my little cherub," he says, wiping tears from his eyes. "You are truly so funny. You almost had even *me* convinced, but of course I knew it to be a prank from the humor you sent down the bond. A wicked prank to be sure, but well done! You should star in the next performance at the theater."

Both of my parents begin to laugh, and no one listens to me when I try to tell them it was not a joke.

When I say there is nothing funny about this and tell them how much he enjoys hurting me, no one listens. The brief moment is gone, and I have gone back to being invisible. Powerless to change my fate.

"You do not have to be powerless, Golden Queen."

The whispers are back, telling me everything I wish to hear. I know responding to the pretend voices would mean I am losing my mind, but that no longer sounds like such a bad thing. I would rather be mindless than exist in this life any longer.

"I do not want to be powerless," I say to the whispers silently in my mind.

"We know a way," the echoing voice respond. I feel too broken at that moment to continue a conversation with an imaginary being that will only give me hope. There is no hope for me. I have been foolish to think otherwise.

The three beings that apparently love me more than any other in the entire realm have decided my life for me. It does not feel true, and if it is, I want no one's love. Not if this is what it looked like.

Maybe I am incapable of being loved.

Dealla

Of Truth & Crowns

The king has finally perished. Not that it means anything good for me. There is nothing in this gods' forsaken palace that is good for me and now I will become queen.

When I first came to the palace to be bonded to the prince, I thought at the very least I could use my station to enact the change I had always been so desperate to see from within the court. Now, I know that will never be possible. I cannot leave the palace and no one will even greet me, let alone discuss politics with me.

The only joy I have found is making the prince's life difficult. I use my shadows to make him trip or fumble in front of others.

The palace is dark enough that no one can see my manipulations. Unfortunately, even that is losing its enjoyment.

I do not know why, but I have never made it apparent to anyone that my magic is shadows. It's a small rebellion and a piece of myself that is for me alone. I love that my bonded has no knowledge of my shadows. It is something I will keep hidden from him until the perfect opportunity presents itself. Perhaps they will terrify him to death. Would that not be fitting for a monster such as him?

Tonight he will become king and I the queen. I can only hope he does not destroy us all during his rule. I wonder what will happen when we sit upon our thrones. The land is meant to speak with each of us. I do not know if that means literally or figuratively, but either way, it will be the first conversation I have had with another in ages. Unless you count the few times per month I spit vitriol at my bonded, which I do not. He is...

I never got to finish my last entry. Suddenly, fae I had never seen before started dressing me for the coronation without saying a word. I thought it funny that a little sparkling crown was set upon my head without much fanfare. Everyone must have forgotten that when a true king and queen sit the throne, the land gifts them their crowns in whatever form it sees fit. However, I knew there would be no blessings from the land with him as king.

I guess I was not entirely correct. The moment our bodies connected with the throne, light shot up all around us. I had been expecting the land to ignore me completely, and judging by the looks of the few fae in attendance, they had been expecting the same. While the voice that was not really a voice should have frightened me, it did not. If anything, I felt comforted for the first time since stepping foot inside this palace.

"Dealla, Queen of the Night Court, though you are more than worthy of the title, I cannot crown you a true queen," it said directly into my mind. "The male you have been forced to bond is not worthy of his bloodline."

"I never wanted to be queen. I never wanted any of this."

"I know. I see everything. You might not have wanted this, but you are where you are supposed to be. I cannot bestow a power on to you, but I can grant you a request."

I thought about seeing my family again, or perhaps just a friend. Until I heard the male growl at whatever the land said to him and I am almost ashamed to admit I wanted him to suffer more than I wanted anything else. There was only ever one thing he wanted, and I wanted to make sure he never got it. I think the land knew what I was going to ask before I did because an eerie sound I think was a laugh filled my mind.

"For every ounce of power he tries to take from another, I want his own power to bleed twice as much away from him. Permanently."

Perhaps I should feel shame for wishing ill on anyone, but I only felt triumphant when the land responded.

"With pleasure. You would have been a wonderful true queen and you deserve much more than the life you have been forced into. Never forget fate knows what is coming and plans accordingly." The final words of the land lingered within my mind as the light disappeared from around me.

He was staring at me and, for a moment, I wondered if he knew what I asked of the land. It did not matter if he did. There was nothing he could do to me. I smiled at him, and his frown deepened.

"Took you long enough. What did it say to you?" he forced the question through clenched teeth. There were moments when I looked at him and thought what a waste of an attractive male, and that was one of them. I am not blind; if only the inside matched the beauty of the outside.

"Not much." It was all I would give him before I stood and gave him a nod before saying, "My king." I said nothing else and walked from the throne room and then ported directly to my chambers to write all of this down.

I do not know why I continue to do so,

but I guess a small part of me hopes a future queen will read these entries and find comfort if they are in a similar circumstance. I suppose writing them brings me a small measure of comfort as well.

Spitefully yours,
Dealla the not true Queen of the Night Court

I live in a daze while preparations go on around me. It is going to happen and there is nothing I can do about it.

"You could. We can tell you how." The whispers in my mind were a special kind of torture. My mind seems to want to torment me with promises to myself I know are impossible to keep. If I truly knew of a way out of this, I would have jumped on it immediately.

I tried to speak to my parents alone. I thought perhaps if he was not there, they would surely listen to me. However, every time I searched them out, it was like *he* knew and got to them before I could.

The bond is no friend of mine.

I know that is how he tracks my every movement and thought. I try so hard to think of nothing, and shut down all of my emotions. Unfortunately, as it turns out, it is nearly impossible to do. Perhaps once I fully mature, it will be a skill I can master.

Too late.

I think this is why he wanted to rush the mating ceremony. He knew I was going to continue attempting to release myself of him and he wanted to fully solidify our bond before that could happen. I see the way the lesser fae look at me. They seem to be the only ones that do. I hate the pity I see in their eyes, even if it makes me feel validated.

I overheard one of them saying something about *"surely he is not expecting her to do the final act yet."* I do not know what this *"final act"* is they were talking about, and I desperately wanted to ask them. A larger part of me is terrified to find out. Now that I am standing before doors that are about to open to the ballroom which has been transformed for the ceremony, I wish I had.

"My darling little ray of sunshine, you look absolutely stunning. Reminold will not be able to keep his hands off of you," my mother says, as if I want *him* to ever touch me again. I glare at her.

"Neither of you ever listened to me and now you are handing me to a monster. I hope before you die you know what you have done." As the final words—a curse—leave my lips, the doors open. My parents stare at me for a moment before sharing some silent conversation above my head.

We begin to walk down the aisle, and I know it is truly too late, but I meant every word. I will never forgive them for this. I want to cry, yet I refuse to give *him* the satisfaction.

I repeat the words the Chronicler tells me to and do the acts the way they instruct, but my mind goes somewhere else. I am not sure I even see what I am doing. The only thing I truly remember is when I reached the end of the aisle signaling the ceremony to begin, but the Chronicler said nothing for a long moment.

I heard murmuring around the room and knew something was not going according to plan. Finally, the Chronicler spoke into our minds.

"A youngling? There has never been a youngling with a fated mate before." I could have hugged the strange, white tree-like being for stating what everyone else seemed to forget. My parents share another look, this one more uncertain. Before they can say anything, if they even were going to, Reminold grabs my hand and yanks me forward.

"I am only here to bear witness and cannot intervene. I am sorry, little one." I knew the words were only spoken into my mind.

"I did not expect to be rescued, but I thank you for seeing the truth."

The Chronicler's final words at the end of the ceremony snap me back to reality. It's one last confirmation that I was not crazy.

"It has been recorded that on this day, Reminold of the Fae Realm's Day Court has bonded Tatiana, the youngling princess of the Fae Realm's Day Court." Reminold's jaw clenches. I know if I have not missed the fact the Chronicler did not say "bonded his mate," then neither has he.

The Chronicler's eyes meet mine, and they give me the slightest of nods before they disappear. I know there is something wrong with my mate bond and I feel like their final declaration has confirmed it. The validation gives me the confidence to meet Reminold's eyes—a mistake I seem to make far too often.

The look I see within their depths promises violence… and something else I cannot name. The small amount of confidence evaporates instantly. His large white feathered wings snap around us and I am filled with the eerie feeling of being caged. Which I suppose I am.

He ports us before anyone, even my parents, can give us well wishes, or whatever is called for in a situation like this. When he snaps his wings behind his back once more, we are in someone's chambers.

I assume they are his.

My stomach begins to twist and flip while every inch of my skin prickles in warning. My intuition screams at me to run, but where would I go? I am forever bonded to him.

"What did that talking tree say to you?" he growls at me while gripping my wrist too hard.

"Nothing." He squeezes even harder. The pain causes me to squeak out the truth. "They said they could not intervene, and that they were sorry."

"What, did you beg them to help you?" he spits as he yanks me toward him.

Every hair on my body stands on end. I do not

know what to say. I doubt he will believe the truth, but I go with it anyway.

"No, I only responded that I had not expected to be rescued." I hate myself a little more every time my voice shakes when I speak to him.

"Nothing can save you from me." He reaches for the neck of my dress and pulls—*hard*. The ripping of fabric and the force with which he pulls makes me fold in on myself and attempt to hide my nearly bare body.

There is no point in doing so.

He gives my undergarments the same treatment, and I stand there naked as he leers at me. I am so cold that my body quakes, but I do not think it is from only the chill in the air.

"What a pretty young female you are becoming." I do not know how I am supposed to respond to that, so I stay silent and stare with wide eyes at the wall across the room. I want nothing more in this moment than to become that wall. "Get on the bed, little cherub."

I do not move.

I am not even sure I heard him correctly. If I was afraid of him before, nothing could have prepared me for the fear I felt now. I have no idea why he would want me to get on the bed, but instinctively I knew he did not want to go to sleep.

He grabs me by the throat with one hand and throws me onto the bed. The action bruising and causing my cries to come out hoarse. Everything around me seems to happen faster than I can comprehend. Yet somehow also moving painfully slowly at the same time, burning every moment into my memory to relive with perfect clarity for an eternity.

His face appears suddenly in front of mine, and he looks like a different being. The anger he wears transforms his face into something hideous. "When I tell you to do something, you do it and say 'yes, my love' with a smile on your face. Do you understand?"

I force myself to nod as the tears pour out of me in rivers down the sides of my face. His hand rears back, and he slaps me so hard I see stars. The cries I had been trying to stifle choke out of me in sobs as I whisper, "yes, my love."

Everything that comes next is a blur of pain and confusion. I shrink myself as small as I can to hide away in the recesses of my mind. I am to be the Queen of the Day Court and yet I am powerless.

"We would never hurt you. We want you to be powerful and able to control everything so that no one could ever hurt you again." If only it were true.

I have no idea how much time passes, but the weight of him finally disappears off of me. I cannot move, even though my mind screams at me to do just that. I want to do nothing. I want to no longer exist.

"Go to your chambers, Tatiana," he says as he pushes me out of the bed. I land hard on my side and yet I still cannot move. "GO!" His voice is a roar that makes my fear greater than my shock. I get up and port to my chambers where I stand, naked and unsure of what I should do.

I reach down to touch something wet between my thighs. When I pull my hand away, it's covered in golden blood—my blood. I do not know what just happened, but I know it should never have happened. Had everyone known this was what awaited me?

I do not remember doing so, but at some point I wrapped a blanket around myself and found the smallest hiding place possible within the room and sobbed. I knew something inside me had died.

Even though I did not know what it was, I mourned it all the same.

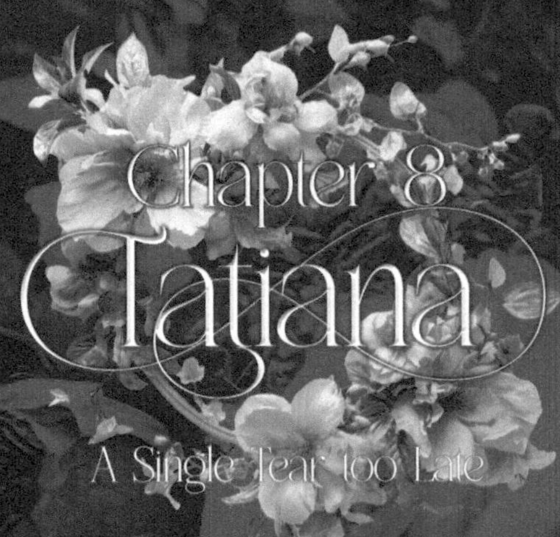

Chapter 8
Tatiana

A Single Tear too Late

Over the years, the echoing voice in the back of my mind has become louder. The constant chatter along with needing to escape my own life has made me unable to tell the difference between what is real and what is not. I have taken to pinching the inside of my wrist to distinguish between dreams and reality.

I refuse to heal myself, or anyone else, for that matter. If I must be broken on the inside, I will be broken on the outside as well. Of course, that does not stop my natural fae healing. I wished it would.

Sometimes I pinch hard enough to draw blood and I stare at the golden liquid as it drips down my wrist. Suddenly, transported back decades ago when I was the youngling crying alone in her room on the night of her bonding ceremony.

I hate when I get stuck in the past more than

being unable to tell my state of wakefulness. At least no matter if I am dreaming or not, I can pretend the past did not happen.

"Golden Queen, let us show you a way to be the most powerful being in the realm." The whispering voices commentated on everything. It's becoming so crowded in my mind; the chaos making it impossible to know my own thoughts from theirs.

For a long time, I thought the voices were my own desires being voiced by my subconscious. Until one day they said something about there being a connection to the elixir Reminold provides and the declining health of my mother. It was something I knew I had never noticed or considered before.

I do my best to ignore the voices whispering in my mind. They frighten me. Who or what they are remains a mystery, but they are incessant. Their promises of power and control are tempting—too tempting. Nothing that sounds that good can be anything but trouble.

Even my young mind knows that much.

It does not help that my dreams waver between visions of ultimate power and ones of past memories I try to bury deeper every day. In my dreams, I can force everyone to do anything I wish and I get to exact my revenge on Reminold and my parents. Watching as they beg me for mercy, even though I know it's not reality, brings me a kind of pleasure I did not know existed.

The other dreams, well, they are the ones that tend to bleed into my waking life. Although I am much older now, Reminold has control over every aspect of my life. It often makes me feel as though I am still that youngling who tucked herself away and cried for reasons she could not understand at the time. That day is impossible to forget when I relive some variation of it every day.

Only now I have stopped crying.

I have stopped everything.

I do not talk to anyone unless it is necessary. It is the one thing I have control over and I use silence as a rebellion against my parents and him. *He* is going to hurt me anyway, so I feel as though I might as well earn it. I do not think my parents have even noticed my silence and faraway stares. They never did truly see me, so I would not expect it to be any different now.

I no longer look at the revolving faces of the fae chosen to instruct me daily. Nor do I even hear them. I spend the entire time staring out the window. I am no longer looking for my friends. They would likely not welcome me, anyway.

I look at nothing as the whispers mix with my thoughts and I find it hard to pick out which ones belong to me and which ones belong to them. I rarely realize I have mutilated my wrist until whichever faceless instructor tries to touch me to pull my hand away from my bleeding limb.

I do not like to be touched.

Particularly when I am stuck in one of my dream-like states. I am sure they mean no harm and yet I cannot help the scream that rips from my lips demanding they not touch me each time. It seems to have the desired effect, for it pulls me back into reality typically to find a small puddle of golden blood on the floor under the wound I continuously open.

My nails dig into my wrist with each pinch, and at some point it opens the skin. While each tiny sting of pain after prevents it from healing. The sight of my blood no longer surprises me. I see it far too often for it to be anything but normal.

A part of me loves the sight of it. The proof that I am, in fact, still a living creature.

A creature.

Not a princess, a high fae, or a being. I am nothing but a hideous creature.

I have never been able to wash away the filth that coated me on the day of my bonding ceremony. It seeped into each pore and filled every inch inside of me, all the way to my bones. There is no escaping it. Only a creature as disgusting as I am would be filled with such putridness. I am rotting away and I only hope it turns me to dust sooner than later.

"You are not a creature. You are the Golden Queen." This is not the first time they have called me that.

"I am no queen."

"You will be." I scoff at the whispers. It's moments like this that make it impossible not to respond.

"I will be nothing but a puppet for my mate." I still cannot say the word mate with anything but vitriol... and fear.

"You do not have to be. Give into us and we will show you how to be the queen you dream of being. We can give you ultimate power. You would have the ability to control everything."

I never respond to them when they start making me promises that I know cannot be true. They—whatever they are—are just another opportunity for disappointment. The list is already long enough, and yet somehow *he* still finds more ways to add to it.

"Tatiana," Reminold seethes. I look up and notice the entire dining room is silent. I forgot where I was.
Again.

His grip tightens around my bleeding wrist. I am certain to others it looks as though he is trying to stop the golden liquid from seeping out. It takes everything in me not to flinch. Somehow I do not feel pain when I am the one inflicting it, yet when it comes from him I feel it ten fold.

He leans in and his hot breath assaults my ear. "Stop marring your skin." The words come out hissed between his teeth so low no other fae ears could hear. "You are embarrassing me. Do I need to remind you of what happens when you are nothing but perfect?"

What he asks of me is impossible for anyone. Not even fate herself is perfect. I made the mistake once of trying to tell him exactly that. It is not one I will make again.

Typically, he is more than happy to hear himself speak, and it's better for me to remain silent. Which suits me just fine. It's the times where he expects a response that I dread. The way his pressure increases on my wrist makes me think this is one of those times.

I don't look to my parents for help.

That would be pointless.

Out of curiosity more than anything, I look at them now. My father barely looks like the fae he was several decades ago. The wine has rotted his mind as much as the filth has me. Yet, nothing compares to the way my mother has wasted away. Each time I lay eyes on her is a shock. She looks as though a gentle breeze could blow her over; the impact turning her into dust before carrying her away.

For the first time in longer than I can remember, my mother and I lock eyes. Perhaps it's the fact that she knows she will be returning to the realm sooner than anyone could have anticipated, but her gaze holds something I have been begging them to for decades. Understanding. She glances down to where his hand tightens even further around my wrist before her eyes flick back to mine.

"Answer me!" His voice seemed to carry further than just my ears when my mother's eyes widen. Tears gather, held back by whatever will she has left. She now knows she gave her daughter to a monster, and it's too late to do anything about it.

The horror I see within her depths makes me happier than I have been in—I am not even sure how long. I hope that when she dies, soon if her current state is any indication, her last thought is regret for what she allowed to happen to me. I smile at her. It is a joyless thing, but it is one that tells her exactly what I am thinking.

A single tear slides down her sallow cheek.

Of Joy & Expectations

It's the strangest feeling, knowing you are creating life within yourself. Strange, yes, but incredible. The moment I knew I was carrying a youngling within me, everything changed.

I stopped caring about trying to make the king's life hell. Honestly, I would have forgotten him entirely if he had not invaded my space, just as his existence faded into obscurity. When I told him I was expecting, I had expected indifference and was surprised to see him genuinely pleased by the news. His reaction would have made me hope for change if it had not been for the worrisome gleam in his eye. I do not know what he is up to, but I do not like it.

The king's brother and his mate returned to the palace shortly after the coronation. I had not even known he had a brother. Apparently, the second he was born, his mother had been instructed to take him away by their father. He only needed one son and she could do as she pleased with the other.

I do not know how she could abandon her first son and wonder if my bonded would be different if he had a mother's love. It is hard to believe anything could have prevented him from becoming the monster that he is. However, one never knows. Either way, it is not worth a moment's thought because there is no changing the past.

When I first approached them, I did so cautiously. I was not sure what to expect, but am pleased to say I at least have two beings I can call friends. The best part is that we will have younglings around the same time. Knowing that my son or possibly daughter will have a friend and cousin to grow up with eases some of the worries I have already begun to foster.

This palace is no place for younglings. The fact they will at least have each other is something. I hope I can give my youngling enough love to balance out the cruelty of their father. A little more weight has lifted off my shoulders knowing they will have an aunt and uncle to look out for them as well.

While I worry for their future, I am excited for mine. I have wanted nothing more than to be a mother and now I finally will be. It is not the male I wished to create a family with, but a family can be a mother and her young as much as any other.

It is a male; I am certain of it. Do not ask me how I know, I somehow just do. I can feel the magic already within him as though my magic calls to his. My shadows recognize his. I already know what I will call him, Ciaran, for he will be my little dark one.

I am determined to create the change I have always desired within the court. There is no better way to do so than raising the crowned prince with kindness, love, and understanding.

He will not become his father. There is not a thing in this realm I will not do to ensure his safety. I only hope that I am enough. *I will have to be. I refuse to let him down.*

> *Expectantly yours,*
> *Dealla — Ciaran's mother*

enough. I will have to be. I refuse to let him down.

Expectantly yours,
Dealla — Ciaran's mother

Chapter 9
Tatiana
The Golden Queen

It's not a surprise when it happens. My mother's end has loomed over her for decades, a shroud of death you could even begin to smell the stench of. I cannot say that I am upset by her death, only that *he* now gets to sit on a throne.

Yes, I will now be the queen and I am supposed to be the ruler of the Day Court. However, thanks to my mate, I am still seen as a youngling, one that is somehow capable of being bonded yet incapable of ruling.

I am tired of being a pawn in everyone else's machinations. I might be young, but I have been forced to grow up quickly by the very ones that seem to think I am incapable of thought.

There is no one to stand in his way. My father disappeared to go on some tour of the realm years ago, not that he would do anything even if he were here. His mind is so far gone to the wine rot I would not be surprised if he got himself killed in some idiotic way. Beyond that, I do not have the power to do so. What would I do? Heal him to death?

If only.

"We have told you there is a way for you to have all the power you desire." The whispers have grown more demanding and harder to ignore. I cannot help but feel what they offer me only makes me a pawn in whatever game they are playing.

I am so very tired. I rarely sleep and my power is having a hard time keeping up between Reminold's constant drain on my well and the abuse. It can do nothing about the dark bags under my eyes. I cannot even enjoy time alone in the sun. *He* always appears within minutes. I wonder, if after he is crowned, will he leave me alone?

Doubtful.

The maids finish dressing me in a gown fit for a queen, so much so I wonder if they pulled it from my dead mother's closet. It looks so much like what she would wear. I do not even have a say in what I will wear when I am crowned queen. I was not even given the courtesy of being consulted.

"All you have to do is listen to us, Golden Queen." I scoff at the whispers and a maid seems to think it was at her. She casts her eyes to the floor and her cheeks redden.

I have no doubts that she has been given direct orders and to listen to none of my demands, if I made any. Not that I would. I know it would be pointless.

I wonder what the palace servants think. Did *he* tell them something to make sure they see me as unfit?

Probably.

I am not even sure that I care anymore. The only thing I desire is to be released from this existence.

"We can show you how to break your shackles."

"At what cost?" I ask them. I do not respond often, but as time passes, it becomes even harder not to.

"There is no cost, Golden Queen." I roll my eyes.

"Of course there is. Everything demands balance. Begone with your lies." My entire life is a lie. I do not have time to listen to any more of them.

The bond is the greatest lie of all. I am certain of it. While it works well enough to confuse my feelings, it is not all-encompassing like I assume it should be.

It is strange to feel an attraction for the being you hate most. I have wondered on many occasions if it would not be easier to just give in and believe the lie he has convinced the rest of the court of.

Maybe I would be able to find happiness. If only I could believe it. Apparently, there is enough of the Tatiana who fought against this mate bond the day it showed up to make it impossible to believe a lie of such magnitude.

I look at myself one last time in the mirror. I never truly look at myself, only the clothing that adorns me. I do not wish to see the creature beneath the garments.

Nothing about what I am wearing is something I

would choose. I sigh and then port to the throne room.

Reminold is already there, giving me one of his many looks of annoyance. I am not late, but I wish I would have thought to be. He cannot do this without me and it would have been my one time to hold power over him.

"You could always hold power over him." I shake my head in an attempt to clear it. Reminold seems to take it personally and grabs onto my wrist, yanking me towards him.

"Stop being a little brat and let's get this over with. I have worked too hard to get to this exact place and you will not ruin it for me. Do you understand?"

Perhaps if he had allowed there to be an audience, I would have heard gasps and maybe even outrage that he dared touch their queen in such a way. Or maybe not. We will never know.

It is customary to allow a mourning period between the death of one queen and the crowning of the other. I could have sat as the crowned princess for hundreds of years, if I desired.

Well, if I had been allowed to desire.

Reminold would not hear of waiting. So now here we are, the two of us and a silent Chronicler, who is only here to observe.

"Do not ignore me!" he screams. I'm shocked when he backhands me across the face and I despise myself for the tears that well. I hate that I still react to his violence. At least I still keep my silence.

"He would never be able to lay hands on you again."

"Sit on the fucking throne, Tatiana." He gives me a shove and I land hard on the giant golden chair, one of two that he had made. One for him and one for me. At least the cushions on the seat soften my landing. Immediately white light shoots up around me, and it's so unexpected I jump slightly.

"Ah, the Golden Queen," a voice that is not a voice says to me, *"you have had a difficult life. Those meant to protect you failed and a larger game has been at play and the ones playing did not care if you were collateral damage."* I feel something wet drip from my chin.

"It is okay to cry, golden one. I can still feel the little princess that was full of fire and bravery. You have tucked her far away. Do not let her disappear. Pull her back out and be the queen you are capable of being. There are two paths fate has determined for you. One will lead to your greatest joy and one will lead to your demise. I cannot tell you anything more. I also cannot give you a gift. The only thing I can give you is your crown of golden sun." I had not been expecting anything at all, but just knowing that the land has seen me the entire time brings a moment of comfort and that is more than most have ever given me.

"What will you give him?" I wish the land would give him a painful death. A sound, I suppose, is meant to be a laugh, reverberates through my mind.

"If only I could, Golden Queen. He will get nothing from me. Your mate is already a thief and has stolen too much from your court. He is a fool to think he tricked fate. Even now, she works to correct his actions. Choose wisely, Golden Queen."

The land is gone before I can ask it what it meant about Reminold. It takes me a minute to register that he is yelling, and it takes me even longer to realize he is yelling at me.

"What did you say to it? You did this." There is a wildness in his eyes I have not seen in decades that makes my throat feel like it's in a vise.

"I -I did not say anything." It's not exactly the truth. I had asked it to kill him. I am not sure if he heard the lie in my words or if he was never going to believe me to begin with.

"It gave you a crown, and it told me I was not meant to have one along with a bunch of other nonsense. So, what did you fucking say?" he bellows as he grips the hair on the back of my head and nearly rips it from my scalp as he forces me to look up at him. "Let's see how hard I have to hit you to knock this fucking thing off your head." His eyes dart to where the crown now adorns me sits.

I glance over to where the Chronicler stood and find the space empty. Apparently, witnessing my humiliation is not a priority for them. Reminold follows my gaze and laughs before he ports us to his chambers.

"You should have just kept your mouth shut when the land spoke to you. But no, you had to ruin what was supposed to be the greatest moment of my life." His hand is still gripped in my hair, and he uses it to slam me into a table with several glass trinkets on it. I feel a few of them shatter under my weight and dig into my skin before he drags me across the table, clearing it of everything.

He throws me into the wall next to it and I cannot help the scream that wrenches from my lungs. I try to keep the words the land told me in my head. I just have to hold on and keep that part of me safe, and then I will finally be rewarded with my greatest joy.

Just hold on.

Hold on.

Hold on.

I am not the slightest bit aware of what I am saying, but I must have begged for someone to help me. Reminold starts laughing as he spreads his wings wide, making him look so much larger.

He bends down to put his face into mine and says, "You stupid whore, there is no one that can save you." He spits in my face before standing up to laugh at me.

As his foot rears back, the last thing I hear before blackness takes me is a whisper in my mind.

"We can show you how to save yourself."

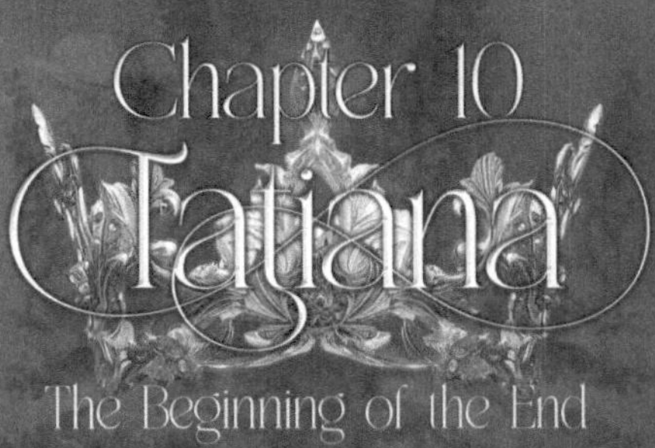

Chapter 10
Tatiana
The Beginning of the End

Has it only been a few years or has it been decades since I became queen?

Time has no shape and is no longer linear when you live the constant loop of the same day. Sometimes I think I stare off and whole days will pass before I come to again. The confusion keeps me in a fog. I think my mind tries to protect itself as best it can by shutting down completely for long periods of time.

In one regard, I am lucky. Ever since becoming king, Reminold has left me mostly to myself. However, sometimes if I am not careful enough and I draw his ire.

I once showed up at a council meeting, wanting to at least know what they were doing with my court. To say he was not pleased is an understatement.

He slowly stood from his seat and said nothing as he approached me. He wrapped his hand around my bicep, noticeably thinner than it had been decades earlier. I may have been much younger, but I had been eating then. I often forget now. His grip tightened and would leave marks that my power would be slow to heal.

He turned to the room and gave them a tight smile. I can only imagine the terror on my face. Sometimes I wonder what the council had thought of that.

I still stood in the doorway, preventing the door from shutting. He dragged me away from it and heard the doors bang shut before he ported us to his chambers. His fists made sure I understood that I was not welcome in the Council Chambers. He left me in a puddle of my own golden blood on the floor and went back to the council meeting as if nothing ever happened.

That was a while ago. When I had been more lucid than not. The whispers spoke to me daily then, but it was not incessant. Now I never have a moment of peace.

The whispers are constantly encouraging me to take back my life. They tell me they can show me how to get my revenge on him. How I can make sure neither he nor anyone else ever touches me again. So many promises and yet they still fail to tell me what the cost would be.

The bond, or whatever it is between us, only makes matters worse. It silently promises peace and true happiness if I just gave in to it. I do not know when it happened, but at some point my traitor heart fell victim to the mate bond.

I love him.

It does not matter that he has, and continues to cause me more pain than anyone else ever has. No, my mate bond whisper pretty lies that convince me he only hurts me because he loves me.

The small sliver of my younger self that still exists rages against the idea. However, she grows smaller and quieter every day while the lies grow louder. Worse still is they have started to not feel like lies anymore.

Is it still a lie if everyone believes it to be true?

What is real?

What is the truth?

Are the whispers to be believed?

What about the mate bond?

I know the land told me all I have to do is hold on to that little piece of me that still lingers and I will be rewarded with true happiness. What if it's a liar too?

How long am I supposed to live like this? Perhaps there are those who are strong enough to take all that life seems intent on giving them. They stand tall and weather the storm that fate has brewed for them. I am just not certain I am one of them.

Let go and embrace your love for your mate.

"Let go and we can bring you true power."

Let go…

"*Let go…*"

Let go…

That little voice of reason, the one that repeats the words *hold on* like its own personal mantra, is fading into obscurity. I hate myself for letting it happen, but at the same time, I am relieved.

Letting go might not lead to the freedom I want, but it will at least lead to my demise. Is that not a form of freedom? I desperately want to know what my true happiness would be, yet I just do not have faith in myself to make it there.

What do I do?

What do I do?

WHAT DO I DO?!

Everything feels like it's spinning out of control, but somehow I see it all crystal clear. I am moving faster than I could port and yet slow, like my limbs weigh twice as much. I am desperate to get some-where, but I do not know where that somewhere is. I forget to breathe and suck in a large breath. My vision blackens around the edges. I see everything *and* nothing at all.

Hold on.

Hold on.

Hold on.

I run with no destination in my mind, but I run to some unknown end anyway. I have to get away, even though it is impossible. When I can no longer breathe. I do not know how far I have run, but when my chest is too tight to take in air, I finally stop.

It's not until I drop to my knees, gasping for air, that I realize where I am. I look around at my favorite meadow of wildflowers. I used to come here often. It was a long time ago when I still had some freedom. A lifetime ago.

Freedom.

I could be free, in a way. Thoughts of surrender battle my mantra to hold on.

"Yes, let go, Golden Queen."

Your mate is your freedom.

Holding on is painful and I am just so tired. I could let go…

"Let go…"

Let go…

I sob into my hands while I listen to the whispers tell me about the power they know I crave.

They know I want absolute control.

They know I want to make sure I am never abandoned again.

They will never do what Glasga, my friends, my mother, and my father have done.

They will never leave me.

I scream at the sun and pull at my hair, trying to rip it from my scalp. I am hoping the pain will bring me clarity.

"I do not want to rule the whole realm. I would be happy to have the Day Court."

Hold on.

Hold on.

Hold...

"*Do not lie to us, Golden Queen. We both know your truest desires.*"

Let go.

Let go.

Let go.

I cannot do it any longer. Oh gods, I cannot do it!

"I am so sorry," I cry out to the land, hoping it is listening. "I know it's the wrong choice of my two paths and I know it makes me weak, but I cannot hold on any longer. I am so tired of being powerless. I am tired of being miserable. I. Am. Tired!" I know it's pointless to try to make it understand.

Part of me cares that the land will be disappointed in me. That is the part I need to fold up as small as possible and lose it somewhere in the darkest recesses of my mind. Somewhere so dark it can never be found again.

She must die. That youngling Tatiana that screams in outrage every time I contemplate giving up. She can be no more. I bury her deep within myself knowing I am giving up on her.

I can pretend that Reminold has always loved me. I can pretend that I have always loved him. I can convince myself that's the truth. My mother's death was nothing more than a tragedy. My father is a selfish male, and I am so lucky to have my loving mate by my side to guide me.

I repeat this as I fold that smallest piece of me remaining away and rewrite my history. I lock it behind wall after wall as I push it further back. Back to the place, things go to be forgotten. My mind knits itself shut over that now dead version of myself.

Let go.

Let go.

Let go.

And so I do.

I let go.

I welcome the whispers into my mind and call them friends.

I welcome my mate into my heart and call him lover.

I feel lighter than I have in I do not know how long and can no longer remember why I was even crying.

I sit up as if waking from a deep sleep and take a deep breath, my lungs fully expanding. I turn my face to the sun, basking in the warmth, and feel at peace.

"We have plans for you, Golden Queen, powerful plans."

The action is foreign after so long, but the unused muscles stretch across my face and I smile.

I am *finally* happy.

Chapter 11
Dealla
Of Pain & Suffering

I watch in horror as my bonded tortures our son. My beautiful boy. He had once been full of wonder and now he's filled with nothing but rage and pain. I cannot say my sacrifice was for nothing, because he still lives.

I scream from inside my mind. I am certain *he* can hear me. The king's face looks far too smug for him not to have.

If only Ciaran could hear me.

All he sees is a mother who sits there silently doing nothing while he's being hurt.

Repeatedly.

I thought the worst was the look on his face when his father made a voice come out of me. Saying whatever he wanted me to, as if I were some puppet.

I was wrong.

The worst was when he stopped looking at me with hope until, one night, he finally stopped looking at me at all. It's worse than any physical torture could ever be.

I can do nothing to protect my boy, and he thinks I choose to do so.

He may look like his father, with the exception of his eyes, but he is all me. I wish there was someone who could tell him that he is not his father. He is his mother who loves him more than the moon.

More than herself.

More than *anything*.

I would sacrifice everyone and everything if it meant I could spare him. My only regret is that I did not do a better job thinking through the wording of our deal. It was hard to think clearly when all I saw was the obsidian blade against his small neck.

Watching as the light I love so much in him turns to darkness always makes me wonder if my shadows would have been faster than his father's blade. In the end, I was not willing to risk his life. The smallest chance he would not survive was too much.

I pray to the gods every night that he knows love in his life. He is owed at least that. I beg them to not make our sacrifices be in vain.

I watch as his father approaches him and applies something to his perfect blue skin. Within a moment, his skin is disintegrating, eaten away by a black substance. I can see the pain in his eyes and I rage against the confines of my mind while my body repeats the movements to sip on the disgusting fluid that keeps me locked away like this and my well open for his use.

The one small satisfaction I have is that every time he steals the power of another, a bit more of his own slips away. I hope one night soon he is powerless and alone, begging for death that refuses to come swiftly.

A tear falls down Ciaran's cheek. I feel the weight of my failure as his mother held within that single tear.

I sob while telling him how much I love him and how proud I am of his strength. The hopes and dreams I have had for him since that very first moment, I held his beautiful little body in my arms. I tell him everything, while begging him to forgive me.

"I am so sorry, my beautiful boy. I am so sorry."

All words he will never hear.

Thanks!

Fancy meeting you here again! I hope you enjoyed your time in the Fae Realm. Perhaps "enjoyed" is not the best choice of word... anyway...

backs away slowly

I've said it before and I will say it again, blurbs and acknowledgements are the hardest things to write! Yet, both are so important. I'm going to keep this one short and sweet, just like the story you just read. Well, maybe not sweet, but you know what I mean.

My family, with extra emphasis on my parents, are wildly supportive. I would not be chasing this dream if they were not standing behind me giving me the space and encouragement to do so. Every single member of my family has sacrificed time with me and not once have any of them made me feel guilty for it. I am truly thankful.

Rebekah and Jess (the hotdog) are my ride or dies. Sometimes we be ridin and sometimes we be dyin but whichever way the day/mood/mental instabilities/ADHD/etc be flowin I know these two are going to be there, no matter where there is. I would have given up at least 69 times if it weren't for them. (They literally would never allow it.)

The rest of the Distracted Inkling fam, Roxie, Kim, Amber, Veronica, Emily, Katherine, and Chelle. I love you all! The way we all support each other and kick each other in the ass to grow is the best. Our late nights and hours upon hours spent together running sprints or… getting distracted… is the best thing to come out of this whole writing experience.

My Chroniclers and Street Team, per usual I am sorry for being a hot mess express! Thank you for cheering me on and supporting me anyway! I want to specifically shout out Amanda. Thanks girl for our chats, I always look forward to them!

Shit. I said this was going to be short, but it wouldn't be complete without thanking you, the reader. These words I tattoo on to dead trees would be obsolete if it were not for you. Thank you for taking a chance on me, and if you're this far in the series, thanks for sticking around! I have so much planned for the Realms and even some side projects coming in the future. I cannot wait to share it all with you.

Love you all!

*This novella has been brought to you by *emotional damage*.*

About the Author

Hi! I'm Amber Thoma, the author of *Prince of Darkness, Heirs of Darkness, and Queen of Light*. I have been a reader for as long as I can remember. I blame personal-pan pizzas (IYKYK) for instilling an obsessive addiction to the many worlds books could take me to early in my life. I grew up in Northern Virginia and lived there until a few years ago, when I moved to a sleepy little college town in the mountains. I live in a 111 year old home with my dog, Lilith, and my cat, Kitten (very original, I know), and I am minutes from my family.

Like many people, lockdown made me reevaluate my life. For over a decade, I knew there was something I needed—a change. I played around with so many ideas. Like moving to a different country, going back to school, and starting a family. None of those felt right. The part of me screaming, "YOU'RE ON THE WRONG PATH," never silenced.

Listening to my intuition when the logical side of

me was smashing the panic button was terrifying. That first step off the path was the most uncomfortable thing I had ever done. They say you have to get uncomfortable if you want to enact real change. Well, I got wildly uncomfortable and uprooted my entire life, and I will never stop being grateful for taking that first step.

If I had never taken that step, I would not have had a year of time with my niece before she suddenly passed away. I would never have taken the time to address my mental health. I definitely would never have sat down and written a book, and committing to a 5 series saga that will take me ten to fifteen years to complete would have completely overwhelmed me. I would have given up before I started, like I have so many times in the past. The folder of several dusty novel plans and intros can attest to that.

What is the moral of the story? Do not let fear keep you from taking that first step off the path you know you are not meant to be on. After all,

Fate gets what fate wants.

Also by Amber Thoma
Prince of Darkness

Realms of Lore: Fae Book One

"She felt as though she were stuck between two impossible choices and almost wished fate would intervene and choose for her."

"Hello pet, you are mine now."

The Night Court's ruling line has been cursed, and a prophecy holds the key. Four beings brought together by the hands of fate must set aside their differences to break a centuries-long curse and unveil secrets that will change everything. Over just a few nights their lives are turned upside down. After all,

Fate gets what fate wants.

Also by Amber Thoma

Heirs of Darkness: A Prince of Darkness Novella

Realms of Lore: Fae Book 1.5

"You must understand, we are wicked creatures, it is our nature. It may not be right, as you have said, but we are what we are."

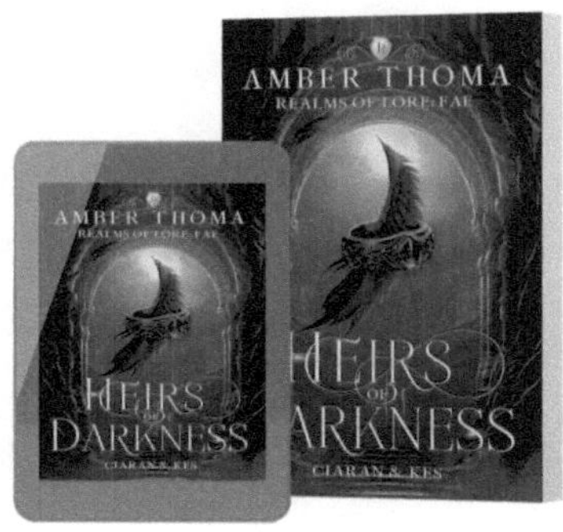

Under the corrupt rule of Ciaran's father, Nightfell Palace is no place for a youngling. Ciaran and Kes are forced to grow up quickly in order to survive the blood soaked paths and tortuous trials set before them. Ultimately, the Night Court will teach them the most important lesson of all…

Fate *always* gets what fate wants.

Also by Amber Thoma
Queen of Light

Realms of Lore: Fae Book Two

"It's okay to be scared, it does not make you less brave."

"I will come for you."

Trouble brews for the fae of the Day Court while witches are hunted in the Boarderlands. Nothing is too far when it comes to love or power. New prophecies are given and promises are made. The beings of the Fae Realm fight for the fates they desire. However...

Fate gets what fate wants.